W9-BNU-872

Equinox

Equinox

Monte Killingsworth

Henry Holt and Company ✎ New York

Henry Holt and Company, LLC
Publishers since 1866
115 West 18th Street, New York, New York 10011

Henry Holt is a registered trademark of Henry Holt and Company, LLC
Text copyright © 2001 by Monte Killingsworth
Illustrations copyright © 2001 by Jennifer Danza
All rights reserved.
Distributed in Canada by H. B. Fenn and Company Ltd.
Library of Congress Cataloging-in-Publication Data
Killingsworth, Monte. Equinox / Monte Killingsworth.
p.   cm.
Summary: Fourteen-year-old Autumn slowly becomes aware of changes
in the tenuous relationship between her father and mother that threaten her
cherished life on a small island off the coast of Washington State.
[1. Islands—Washington (State)—Fiction.   2. Fathers and daughters—Fiction.
3. Mothers and daughters—Fiction.   4. Artists—Fiction.
5. Washington (State)—Fiction.]   I. Title.
PZ7.K5575 Eq 2001   [Fic]—dc21   00-54399

ISBN 0-8050-6153-3 / First Edition—2001 / Designed by Donna Mark
Printed in the United States of America on acid-free paper. ∞
1   3   5   7   9   10   8   6   4   2

for Maya

There is no change but this change,
equinox; a sweetening of time,
like salmon or rain.

Equinox

Thirty and higher,
The air is very dry;
Below twenty-nine,
Clouds will surely fill the sky.

A slow steady drop,
Expect foul weather;
The barometer sinks lowest
For wind and rain together.

Sunday

sunday morning

low tide: 8:07 a.m.
barometer: 29.32; falling

I return to the forest and suddenly everything seems much more important: the yellow light, the sky, shadows dancing with the breeze. And behind me, the bay.

I knew change was coming.

⚶

Forrest came three times during the week and stayed late. I lay upstairs and listened to them talk. Their voices were low and they didn't laugh.

I was surprised to see Mother's boat come into the bay on Thursday—a day early. Because of the weather, she said, though the sea was calm and the sky blue. Friday, Mother and I worked in the herb garden and then we made oatmeal cookies and cleaned the house together. Harley worked all day in his shop. I looked out there once in a while and saw him piling tools and stuff outside the door.

I knew something was going on.

For as long as I can remember, Harley and I have

lived in a little log cabin down by the bay. Mother lives with us, too, but she goes to work on the big island— San Juan Island—every Monday morning and comes back on Friday afternoon. During the week she takes a hot bath at dawn, drinks espresso in a café, works late, and has a lot of meetings, then goes out to dinner with friends. These are things she can't do here.

Mother has converted her office into a studio apartment with a folding futon, a little kitchen (kitchenette, she says), and a tiny deck with a view of the harbor. All around her apartment are watercolors of flowers she's painted, pots she's made, and books.

Mother isn't exactly like Harley and me.

❦

What Harley likes to do best is work in his shop. From September to May, he is out there pretty much every day. He makes little wooden things like combs, barrettes, and mirrors. Sometimes he makes jewelry boxes and tables. And every year he builds a few dulcimers and rocking chairs.

All his projects come from wood he finds on the island. It's sort of like recycling. Harley's boxes, dulcimers, and chairs were once fence posts, broken tree limbs, firewood, or roots. If someone tears down an old shack or has some scraps from building a house or if a piece of yew turns up in a woodpile, you can bet Harley will be there soon, looking at the wood in his special way. Wandering around and gathering interesting pieces of wood is also one of Harley's favorite things to do.

Mine, too.

In the summer, Harley and I travel and sell all the stuff he makes. Almost every town in Washington, Oregon, and Idaho has a crafts fair or an art show and that's where we go. Uncle Bob lets us use his pickup to pull our trailer because we don't have a car or truck of our own. In every town where we set up our booth, Harley puts on his jester outfit and begins to juggle or do acrobatic tricks, and people come to buy. I work behind the counter, taking money and making change. The customers nearly always say the same things: "I've never seen wood this beautiful. Where'd you find it?" And, "That's your dad, isn't it? Boy, you two sure look alike." I suppose we do, in a general sort of way. Skinny. Not too tall. Blue eyes. Freckles. Blondish hair (Harley's is more red).

By the end of summer the mirrors and jewelry boxes and chairs are all sold, the money box is full, and it's time to go home.

I love this, this circle of our life. It's a special, simple, quiet way to live.

But now everything is different.

I thought at first maybe Mother was going to have a baby. They talked about it a long time ago, once, when I was supposed to be asleep. A brother or sister for Autumn is the way Harley put it. Now that I'm fourteen it seems a little late, but it did enter my mind, especially with Mother tidying up the kitchen and baking cookies and all that.

Then I started to think Mother was really going to quit her job at the Whale Museum. It's something she says, although I don't think Harley takes her any more seriously than I do. Mother likes to paint and make pottery and work in the garden. She's taught herself to play the dulcimers Harley makes, and last year she traded some of her pottery for a harp. She loves to write and to walk, alone, down by the sea. Most of all, Mother loves to read. Our house is filled with books and she has read every one of them.

Now and then Mother says she ought to just quit her job and write at home so she'd have more time for the things she loves. The museum is too hectic, she complains, and it's getting too big.

Harley and I usually give each other a look. Partly because she's been saying the same thing for years and mostly because we know Mother and—let me put it this way—there are exactly zero espresso shops on our island and about the same number of bookstores. And nobody, especially Harley and me, could imagine the Whale Museum without Mother or Mother without the Whale Museum. They just go together. Anyway, I thought about her being here every day and didn't like the idea as much as I should have.

I guess I was afraid everything might get all messed up. Harley is the world's easiest person to get along with and he lets me be who I am. It goes the other way, too. I sometimes make Harley something for lunch and take it out to him in the shop so he won't forget to eat. And I don't mind if he has sawdust in his ears or wears the same shirt all week or listens to Grateful Dead records real loud. I don't mind if he tells me stories I've heard before about when he was young and rode his motorcycle (that's where he got his nickname). I wasn't sure I wanted to give up the long weeks together, even if it meant I'd see Mother more.

I look out across the bay. A little red-and-white Piper seaplane lifts off the green water and banks hard to the east. A gull struts around on the dock, picking at the old wood, looking for something to eat. The dock rises and falls as the wake from the Piper slants in. A few big clouds move slowly across the sky; a steady breeze blows out of the south.

I'm cold just sitting here so I decide to walk. I slide down the silver stump, pick up my stick and backpack, and start down the trail. Soon I'm out on the southern headland, high above the sea. Out here in the open, at the very edge of land, with the wind in my face, I let myself think about what Harley said at breakfast.

"It's time we left the island," his words hanging in the air. For some reason, I try to remember what my face did at that moment. Harley probably practiced that sentence so he could get it right; it's not something he would ordinarily say.

A strange, thin cloud formation has appeared now along the western horizon, and far out to the south there are white lines on the water, moving with the current. I think about Harley's voice. It sounded strange and hard.

The weather is changing; something is coming in.

"It's time we left the island."

I remember I turned to Mother. That was the worst thing. I turned without thinking because she and I can change Harley's mind about anything. I turned to her for help and saw . . . nothing. That was the awful part— her face was blank. Anything would have been better than that. Crying, yelling, holding my hand. Anything. But she only shrugged and sipped her tea. "I can be happy whatever you decide," she said. "It's up to you and your father."

❦

Our house is far behind me now, out of sight. There's only the narrow trail, the dark cliffs, the sea, and the sky. Harley and Mother are probably washing dishes. It's a weekend ritual, a chance for them to talk. I've seen them do it a thousand times, I can see them in my mind now. They're talking about me, about moving away. Harley is washing; he's concerned; he's wondering if this is the right choice. Mother dries and reassures him as she places each dish exactly where it belongs. She calms him, talking sensibly in her slow deep voice.

I wonder if it's Mother's idea and not Harley's.

There are some things you don't have to think about, things that are simple and solid. Leaving the island is one of those.

I'm walking on the southernmost point of the island now, more than a mile from our cabin. As I round the point I come face-to-face with open ocean and a strong steady wind out of the west. And I see Forrest some distance away, moving toward me on the trail.

sunday afternoon

high tide: 2:13 p.m.
barometer: 29.18; falling

Forrest knows more about Douglas Island than anyone. He's been here for a very long time. He lives alone at the lighthouse on the west side, in a tiny white cottage high on a bluff overlooking the strait. He doesn't exactly run the lighthouse; it's all automatic now. When he tells people he's the caretaker, Forrest means he takes care of the lighthouse itself, like painting and keeping the glass clean. Truth is, Forrest is caretaker for the whole island. He fixes generators, heals pets (and people sometimes), patches boats, keeps the trails clear, predicts storms, and always seems to be there when he's needed.

Like now. I need someone to talk to and here he is. His white hair blows around his head as he approaches. He leans against a rock, his blue eyes smiling.

"Hello, Autumn. Shall we sit?" Forrest grew up in Maine. I never know if his accent disappears or I just stop hearing it. I sit on a rock across the trail from him.

"So. You're planning to leave us." Harley has obviously told him.

"Not me," I say. "*Harley's* planning to leave, though I can't imagine why."

Forrest's eyes sparkle. "And your mother?"

"She says she doesn't care, that she can be happy either way, leaving or staying. She's letting Harley decide. Mother spends most of her time on the big island anyway, so it wouldn't be such a change for her."

"She's ambivalent," Forrest says matter-of-factly.

"I suppose so." (I've learned a lot of new words from Forrest.)

"And what about you?" he asks. "You can't stay here if your parents leave."

"No," I have to agree, "I can't stay here alone."

Forrest smiles, just a little.

"But I can't leave either."

"Well, I suppose not," he says. "I mean, just like that." He snaps his fingers. "I imagine it'll take some getting used to, living over there after all the years you've been—"

I cut him off. "I *can't* leave, Forrest!"

"I see." He looks past me, at the water. The little smile is gone. "What will you do?" he asks.

"I don't know. I'm still thinking about it."

We're silent for a while. With his white hair and bushy beard, Forrest looks like Santa's thinner hippie brother. Today he's wearing a flannel shirt buttoned to the top, a pair of chino pants, a sports coat, and a string tie. And Birkenstock sandals, as usual. He's a pretty snappy dresser. Of course, I'm used to Harley, whose entire wardrobe is made up of jeans and T-shirts. I study the slider on Forrest's tie and decide it's supposed to be a raven. Behind him the dry grass leans away from the wind.

"Let's have some lunch, Autumn. I've made soup."

Forrest's Pacific Soup is famous on the island—everybody loves it. In this recipe there's food from his garden, from the forest, and from the ocean—carrots, potatoes, garlic, mushrooms, mussels, seaweed, and more. Nothing from the store. That's the whole idea. Forrest goes for a walk with his basket and when he comes home he puts it all in the pot.

I taste the broth. Delicious. It's hot, so I spread butter on a thick slice of bread and wait. There's the ocean smell of the soup, the warm bread, the ticking of the clock. And elderberry jam in a blue china bowl.

"You know," Forrest says, digging into his soup, "one

of the reasons Harley wants to move is to give you a better education."

"You don't really think I can get a better education over there. In some huge school with a bunch of city kids?"

Forrest looks away, spoon in hand. "Harley's thinking about next year, about high school. He's real proud of all those straight-A report cards, always talking about how smart you are." Forrest looks me in the eye. "But smart isn't quite the right word, is it? Lots of kids are smart. You're a bona fide observer of the world, Autumn—with a practiced eye—and a deep thinker, too. On top of that, you have a way with words and a steady hand. A girl like you just isn't going to get everything you need at the school here. You know what I mean."

"You could help me."

"Yes. I told Harley that. And I also told him you seemed to be doing fine. You're taking the usual school subjects, but you're learning about the outside world, too: plants, animals, tides, weather. I doubt you'll get much of that on the big island."

"That's for sure. I've seen the school over there; it looks like a penitentiary." Forrest smiles.

"Harley's convinced you need to go to the high school, so you can get ready for college."

"Yeah." Harley never went to college. "He's pretty set on me going."

"He's kind of talked himself into it, if you follow my drift. Harley was more interested in his motorcycle than school. He wants you to get the kind of education he missed. And he's sure you can't get it here."

I try to guess where Forrest is going with this. Island kids probably don't go to college. I mean, I don't know where they go when they leave. If they leave. Right now, college is about the last thing on my mind. I put jam on a second piece of bread. I don't think school is the main reason Harley wants us to move anyway. I think it's something else.

"Maybe you should start keeping a journal," Forrest says, sliding a flat package across the table.

I hunch into my jacket. The sky is silver, and there are long wisps of clouds in from the west. The tops of the trees move in the breeze. The air is cool.

I'm sitting cross-legged in my second-favorite thinking place and from here I can see our cabin below. Mother's inside, sitting in her corner chair, reading a magazine. Harley's making a stack of stove wood under the eaves next to the rose trellis. Sidecar, our golden retriever, follows him back and forth from the woodpile to the house.

This place has been my home for as long as I can remember—this cabin, this island, the big cookstove warming the kitchen, the old cedar log walls silvery now in the fading light.

I don't care about college and I don't care if we're only renters and I don't care if Harley doesn't make much money and I don't care if there aren't many kids on the island. None of that matters to me.

I see Mother shift in her chair to allow more light to fall on her magazine. It's different for her. If she lived on the big island she wouldn't have to take the *Wind Spirit* across the strait every week, she could be home at night, and she'd be close to town. Over there she could still make pots, paint, write, read, and have a garden. Everything Mother loves about this place can be taken with her. She doesn't love the island deeply, not the way Harley and I do. She just lives here.

Evening falls. Our cabin glows as the sky and land darken around it. From time to time, Harley stops and looks down the trail for me.

I'm almost ready.

The journal Forrest has given me rests easily on my lap. The light is thick and green on the page. The pen glides. I draw; I write a few words. I take my time. I try not to think about every line. I don't want this to be perfect—I want to look at this page tomorrow or next week or when I'm an old woman and be very sure that what I see then is exactly how I'm feeling right now.

Monday

monday morning

low tide: 8:46 a.m.
barometer: 29.04; steady

I awaken in darkness to the sound of wind. I throw off the quilt and dress quickly in the dark. There's a faint blue line southward; it'll be light in half an hour and Mother will go.

From the top of the stairs I feel the warmth of the cookstove and smell hotcakes and coffee. Harley and Mother hear the stairs squeak and say, "Morning, Autumn," at the same time and laugh.

Mother sits at the table, dressed for work in a simple cotton dress, tights, and boots. Her black hair is long, and this morning it's wet and brushed back tight. Her reading glasses make her look older, even though she's only thirty-two, ten years younger than Harley.

"Morning," she says again, looking up at me from her paperwork. She's smiling. Mother takes off the glasses and holds out her arms. "There you are. I didn't want to wake you." I lean into her. I smell her skin, the slight scent of lavender. "But I really wanted to see you before I left. You were gone so long yesterday," she finishes.

"I figured you went to the lighthouse. I saw you heading that way," Harley says. I kind of hold my breath, hoping he doesn't mention anything about leaving the island. He's leaning against the stove, coffee cup in hand, keeping an eye on the hotcakes. "Forrest say anything about this weather coming in?"

I shake my head and murmur, "No." I don't want to talk about the weather or about leaving. I squeeze Mother and take my place. Our table is a corner booth out of an old Seattle diner, with an L-shaped candy-apple-red metal flake tuck-and-roll vinyl bench. I slide in and sit on the long side. From here I can look out the big picture window. It's starting to get light.

"Well," Harley says, "feels like the wind is picking up a little to me. Kinda chilly in here, isn't it?" This is supposed to be a joke: it's warm as toast in the kitchen. He puts the hotcakes on a platter and carries it theatrically, balanced on his fingers, to the table. "Breakfast is served," he says, with a sort of English accent. Harley grabs a cup of coffee and slides into the booth next to Mother.

There is no more talk of weather and nothing is said about moving or leaving.

Mother eats carefully and slowly and sometimes listens to Harley and me while she looks at her paperwork. Harley wolfs down six or seven hotcakes covered with warm maple syrup and around five cups of coffee, all the while talking about the table he's making out of some oak boards. It's amazing all the things Harley can say about a table. I keep him going on the subject so he won't suddenly decide to talk about something else, and I tell him a little about my visit with Forrest yesterday.

And then it's time for Mother to go.

We listen to the weather band on the radio (wind twelve to fifteen knots out of the southwest) before walking to the dock. I remember my journal and run back to get it as Harley and Mother continue slowly down the trail. I catch up to them easily. They talk about their week: Mother has a big grant to write; she'll be working late every night. Harley's going to finish the oak table and clean out his shop. He says nothing about leaving, but I hear it in his voice.

The tops of the mountains are golden with morning sun. The trees rustle in the breeze, but the bay is smooth as glass. The only thing moving down here is us. As Harley steps onto the dock a little ripple moves out across the water, disturbing the stillness.

Mother's boat, *Wind Spirit,* is a nineteen-foot 1955

Chris-Craft Capri, her pride and joy. It's a two-seat runabout, made entirely from wood. There's nothing else like it in the bay. Even Harley likes it. It's kind of an antique and a hot rod all in one. It had been her great-uncle's boat; he left it to Mother in his will. Mother says it was because she was the only relative who lived near water. When her uncle died they hauled it up here from California. I was too little to remember, but I've heard the story a hundred times: Harley leading the way on his motorcycle, Mother driving the rented truck, the big trailer, people waving from cars.

Far down the bay is the other dock, and there's Jane, waiting, silhouetted against the white morning sky.

Jane moved here two years ago from the big island. Her father—who's rich, I guess—had a little cabin built for her near the southern tip of the island. The cabin has a rock fireplace, big windows, and a great sunny view to the south. Jane's twenty-three and works at the Whale Museum as an intern, doing research. This means that unlike Mother she spends a lot of time out in boats actually studying the orca whales.

Jane is small and she smells like sandalwood. She gives me clothes that she doesn't wear anymore, loans me magazines, and lets me sit on her deck and talk about anything.

On a calm day, Mother can cruise from our island to Friday Harbor in just under fifteen minutes. Today there'll be wind and chop, so it'll take a lot longer than that. Mother will pick up Jane, and they'll walk down to the boat and climb in. Mother will open the throttle and they'll be off.

"This isn't easy for me," Harley finally says, breaking the silence. His back is to me; he's watching *Wind Spirit* down the bay, leaving a long wake in the black-and-gold water. "I don't know if she can be happy with only us." I try to put Harley's words out of my mind.

By mid-morning I'm back at the lighthouse.

"Well, he's thinking about a lot of things," Forrest says. "But mostly Harley wants you to go to school, he wants your mother to be happy, and he wants his family to be together. For him that adds up to a move to the big island." For a moment, I think about Harley standing straight and alone on the dock, watching the *Wind Spirit* disappear.

"Mother often says that she should quit her job and just stay here and write full-time."

Forrest brings two cups of tea from the kitchen. Then he stands precariously on a chair and begins to pull some books from a shelf above his desk. He says without turning around, "And paint those little watercolors and grow a lot of herbs and make raku pottery and travel around with you and Harley in the summer and sell all that stuff and make more money than she does at the museum and"—Forrest steps very slowly off the chair, holding several large books, and turns to look at me—"she would not have to eat at restaurants and buy all those clothes for work and fire up that Chris-Craft every Monday and run it over to Friday Harbor and then she could save a lot of money and life would be good, right?"

I smile. This is exactly what Mother says, pretty much word for word. Like me, he's heard it many times.

I sip my tea. Tea is another wonderful thing Forrest makes. He collects mint, grasses, and berries during the summer, dries them, and crushes them for tea. This one tastes like blackberries and flowers.

"That's what she says, but do you think she'd really be happy if she never left the island, if she were here every day?" He arranges a stack of books on the table between us and begins to fill his pipe.

"No," I answer. "Harley's right. Mother could never live on this island like we do. She'd go crazy."

"Yeah," Forrest says quietly, "she probably would."

We're silent. Outside, far below, is a pattern of wind on the sea and a stormy sky to the south. The little cottage is filled with morning sun. A fire crackles in the woodstove. Something is cooking in a silver pot, making the lid dance.

It's just one room, with a counter between the kitchen and the living area, and a loft for sleeping. Forrest's lighthouse cottage is tidy and scrubbed. It's filled with books and a lifetime's collection of shells, rocks, glass floats, and driftwood, carefully arranged on the shelves and windowsills. The south and west sides of the house are mostly window. The other walls are covered with pine, turned golden with age. The floor is made from pieces of dark stone.

Sometimes I think about the lighthouse keepers years ago who lived here alone, when there was nobody else on the island. I imagine them coming into the

cottage out of a storm and sitting on this very bench at this very table, watching the sea below as I'm watching it now. What did they think about? What were they like?

They were a lot like Forrest, I suppose. But at least Forrest has us—Harley and me—and others on the island. He walks around; he visits people; he goes to Friday Harbor once in a while.

"You brought your journal, then?" Forrest says through his pipe-clenched teeth.

It's next to me on the bench, so I hand it to him across the table.

Forrest finds the reading glasses he wears around his neck, puts them on, and studies the first page for a long time. He moves his finger along the words I've written and over the drawings of our cabin. He looks up at me over his glasses as he turns the page. He studies the drawings of the bay and the *Wind Spirit* in the same way. I'm worried he's not going to like them.

I look around the cottage and wait. It smells like black beans cooking in the pot. And Forrest has a lot of new herbs, garlic, and other plants hanging from the beam in the kitchen to dry.  Mother says he's the best cook on the island and I believe it. He seems to know about everything. He knows about the currents in the strait, about stars and weather and animals, and he knows more about the history of this island than anyone. Harley calls him the medicine man of our tribe.

Forrest is older than my parents, but he's not so old. I mean, he can walk a lot faster than I can and when he and Harley split firewood, Forrest always splits the most. He taught at a college somewhere in California until he got fed up with paperwork, as he says, and came here. Now he makes his living as a freelance artist. That's all I know about Forrest and I suppose that's all anyone knows.

He's short and thick and has a round face mostly covered with a white beard.

"You have a knack, Autumn," he says, looking up. "This is indeed a journal."

Music to my ears.

"Now let me show you the journals I kept when I was your age."

❦

The light moves across the table. We drink our tea and I look through his dusty journals one by one.

With a few pen strokes and just the right words, a moment is captured; this is what I've tried to do. And here it is, page after page, right in front of me.

Forrest smokes his pipe and watches me. There is no need for explanation; the journals speak for themselves.

There's a snake he caught and kept in his room. There's a field, sloping down to a river, the evening shadows long, and a stick fishing pole leaning against a tree. There's a barn, and on the next page an old cook-stove with two pies cooling on top. And there is Forrest's house in the winter, blue tracks across the snow. Everywhere there are birds, and flowers, and shadows and light, and words to hold it all together.

Not many words, only the important ones:

> *Blackberry and peach pies for dessert.*
> *Ten below zero, fox got three chickens.*
> *Chickadee.*
> *Hollyhocks.*
> *Grandpa's grave.*
> *Mom's camellia, Feb.*
> *Broken fence down by creek.*

And after I've looked through all the pages—one book from each year of Forrest's life from ten years old to seventeen—it's early afternoon and time to go.

Forrest waves from the door of his cottage as I climb the path toward home and I wave back.

monday afternoon

high tide: 2:52 p.m.
barometer: 28.91; falling

When I get home, Harley's in his shop. I can hear the rasp-rasp-rasp sound of one of his little saws and then the strange rumbling of the treadle sander. I wait in the yard. Sidecar gets up from his place by the shop door and comes out to greet me. I scratch his ears. When the sander stops I yell, "I'm home."

Harley sticks his head out the door. He's wearing goggles and a ragged baseball cap that says Mac Tools in faded letters. He's covered with yellow sawdust. "Hi, sweetie. Make a sandwich if you want. I'll be in later."

I decide to eat lunch and then take a shower. I find the hummus in the pantry and make two sandwiches, one thin and one real thick, with onions. I put the thick one on a plate with some potato chips and take it out to the shop.

"Lunch."

Harley is pleased. "Thanks," he says. I turn quickly and walk back to the house so he won't feel like he needs to talk to me. He has work to do and so do I.

· 33 ·

I eat out on the front porch, listening to the wind in the trees. The air is bright and filled with autumn light. The branches of the big Douglas firs sparkle as they move about. A couple of buzzards circle around. I finish lunch, tidy up the kitchen, and head to the back porch to bathe.

There's no electricity on Douglas Island. Like everyone else, we have an outhouse instead of an inside toilet. Our water comes from a spring up on the mountain behind our home and flows into a tank buried in the ground near the kitchen. A pitcher pump on the sink draws it out of the tank. There isn't much water, so we have to be very careful. If we need hot water, we heat it in a kettle on the woodstove.

We don't have a bathroom. Mother sponges herself off at the kitchen sink when she's here. Harley and I take showers on the back porch.

Here's how it works: Harley has a big black plastic bag he fills with water and puts out in the sun. In a few hours, the water is hot and he hangs it from a pulley on the back porch. There's a nozzle at the bottom of the bag with a spigot to turn it on and off. Beneath the shower there are slats in the floor and beneath the slats is a big flat metal pan that catches the water and runs it through a hose to the flower bed beside the house.

I flip the spigot. The water is almost hot. I turn it off while I scrub myself, then use as little water as possible to rinse off. I try to enjoy this as much as possible: a month from now neither the water nor the porch will be nearly this warm. Wrapped in a towel, I check to see that there is enough water left for Harley. Only Harley can lift down the black bag to fill it and I don't want to disturb him. I want to walk around and look at things. Write and draw. Think.

I want to be alone.

I find an old gray log near the water and sit down. I sharpen my pencil and consider moving to the big island. The more I think about it, the more it doesn't make sense. It seems like Harley's got this idea stuck in his head.

I'm sketching the bay. Forrest says if I do a good job on this journal and sort of leave it around for Harley to find, he'll see how much I already know about animals and plants and stars and tides and drawing and writing and he might begin to change his mind about school.

Forrest thinks Harley doesn't really want to move anyway, and it wouldn't take all that much to get him rethinking the whole idea.

Me, I'm not so sure. It seems like a long shot. I figure Harley must have been thinking about this for a while.

I decide to draw the island itself. I start with the line where the land meets the sea, then add the slickrock and the tide pools, the forest, firs and madrones and oaks. And the path going around the island. The path is open and sunny and high above the water on the south side, dark and shady as it winds through trees on the north.

There's the long bay and the boats and our log cabin up on the rise. The old couple's vacation house down closer to the bay, and Jane's cedar cottage, and the other houses all along the south side, the lighthouse, and the school. A landing strip on the east side; the orange wind sock, the planes tied down.

The old homestead, the barn fallen down, the gray picket fence around what was once a yard. The old road cutting through the middle of the island, from the logging days, grown over with moss and ferns now.

Asters on the sunny hillsides, and mushrooms where it's cool, and lichen on the alder trees that grow by the shadowy creek.

Geese and swans that fly over in the spring and fall, and orcas, sea stars, and owls.

Wind and cold and ice, and sparkling water and dark sky, and autumn, and spring, and the smell of apples and sunflowers.

I don't want to leave anything out.

I finish the map and load everything in my backpack. By the time I get to the lighthouse the sky is gray and the tide is in.

Forrest is reading in the big chair by the south window, smoking his pipe. There's a fire in the stove and the smell of baking bread. A few madrone leaves blow in through the door with me.

Forrest looks up from his book. "Something coming in, isn't there?" It's been hot and dry for a long time.

"Yes, it's pretty windy out there," I say. "The weather's changing."

"Barometer's dropping. There'll be a storm by the end of the week, I think. Rain more than likely." Forrest rises and carefully places the book facedown on the chair. I notice it's a book about plants.

"How are you getting along with your journal?" he asks. "May I see?"

We sit at the table and look together at what I've done so far. Forrest nods and moves his finger over the pages.

"Good, very good," he says. "Your journal has heart; I don't think anyone can teach you that. But you might want to get more focused. May I show you something?"

Forrest moves pen over paper without touching down, making a pattern in the air while he talks.

"Here is your cabin, more or less." With a few strokes Forrest draws our house. It's perfect. "And here's my house." The same thing, zip-zip-zip, and there's the lighthouse with the attached cottage, the door standing open, the fir trees on the ridge leaning away from the wind.

"Now, think about my old journals I showed you and the drawings you've done." He taps the sketches he's just completed. "How are they different?"

I want to say that mine aren't as good as his but that's not what he means and it doesn't matter anyway.

There's a difference but I can't think what it is. "I don't know," I tell him.

"Imagine the drawings you've made as photographs," he says, "and tell me, where's the camera?"

Suddenly I understand what he means. "In my drawings I'm far away."

"Yes, you seem to be drawing the things in your life from a distance—"

"But I *was* at a distance when I drew them. I was sketching what I saw."

He smiles. "In a journal you're recording your experience. It's more than a collection of drawings."

I don't get it, exactly.

"Think about your mother's boat for a minute," he says. He opens my journal to the sketch of Mother leaving this morning. "This is a fine drawing, Autumn. I love the wake lines and the dock. You've captured the moment, no doubt about it. But think about the boat itself."

Forrest moves the pen around in the air for a moment, then makes a sketch of several boats out on the water, two gulls, and a little dock. "You've grown up with that boat, right?" I nod. "How many times have you been aboard?" Thousands, I want to say, but that's probably too many.

"Hundreds, I guess."

"And you've walked your mother down on Mondays for—"

"—as long as I can remember," I finish, "and met her on Friday afternoons."

"So, if this was the only sketch of the *Wind Spirit* you had twenty or fifty years from now, what would be missing?"

I peer at the drawing. "Which one is the *Wind Spirit*?"

Forrest smiles. "That's the whole point. You're often a lot closer to it. Something like this."

I watch him draw a curve that becomes most of the front deck and three lines that become the windshield. Then the steering wheel and the tie-up cleat, the running lights, the seats, and even the grain of the wood.

Finally he draws the edge of the dock, and a coiled rope, and it's as though I'm there.

"This is more like how you know the *Wind Spirit,* am I right?" he asks.

"Yes," I have to agree. "Forrest, how do you do it?"

He laughs. "Well, it just takes practice. I've been working at this for a long time. And I love that boat, by the way; that helps. I've sketched it many times. But the point is, look at what's happened to the distance."

He's right. This is better. The boat is so close and real, I can almost reach out and touch it.

"Details are important, Autumn, and you should include them in your journal when you can. Distance is okay, too, and I love the map, but sometimes you'll want to get closer, that's all."

He takes a small pen from a wooden box with a sliding top. I recognize the box—Harley made it. He holds out the pen and winks.

In my hand, the pen is heavy and cool. Forrest takes the pen from me and makes a quick sketch of a leaf, then draws a stem with a blossom just opening, then two more, fully open.

It's a wild rose. In just a few seconds he has drawn one of my favorite plants; no one could mistake it for anything else. He winks again. Forrest shades in the leaves with some dots, draws a few detail lines, and it's done. He holds out the pen.

"Me?" I ask awkwardly.

He turns over the sketch of the *Wind Spirit* and the rose. I take the pen and try to copy an aster from the book Forrest was reading. Too fat. I try again. He watches me with narrowed eyes. The second one isn't right either. I look at Forrest. He nods, just a little. I try again. And again. Each try is worse than the last. After the fifth try I place the cap on the pen and lay it on the table. We wait together in silence for someone to say something.

"You're trying to draw too much," Forrest says finally. He picks up the pen. "What is the important thing about an aster? The shape and arrangement of the leaves and the bloom, right?" He makes a quick sketch. I hope he doesn't expect this to help me feel better.

"See? Two blooms with their little rays shooting out from the center and a few narrow leaves sticking this way and that off the main stem. No one could mistake this for a rose or thistle, could they?"

I shake my head. I've already decided I'll never draw again.

"The trick is to get the sizes and shapes right. You don't have to draw the whole plant, just like I didn't need to draw the whole boat for you to recognize the *Wind Spirit*. It needs to be very simple, just the barest outline. The viewer's eye will fill in the rest."

The sky is dark; it's nearly evening. I can hear the breakers washing over the rocks below. With the journal and Forrest's pen safely tucked away in my backpack, I make my way along the path, down to the bay and home.

Late that evening Harley knocks on my door, and I let him call out my name twice before answering. He always raps on the door frame and waits to be invited in, even when the door's wide open like now. "Come in, I'm awake."

"Howdy, Autumn."

I sit up and wrap the blankets around my shoulders. Harley pulls over my rickety wooden chair and sits in it backward like he always does. He lights the candle on my table, and yellow light fills the room.

My room is on the south side of the house. Harley built the room when I was three. He just cut out a big chunk of the old roof and put up some walls and a new roof. He jokes about it: "More like a big dormer than a room, isn't it?"

But I love this room. There are big windows on three sides, with window seats. Between the windows are logs Harley cut and peeled himself. The cracks are chinked with white clay he found on the north side of the island.

There's a skylight over my bed that opens with a crank so I can let heat out in the summer. The floor is made from old oak boards Harley got from a barn. The stairs are split logs curving down into the main part of the house.

"Are you sure you're awake?" he asks gently.

"Yeah," I say, "I'm awake." I notice he's freshly scrubbed and has on a clean flannel shirt. His hair and beard are still wet. In the candlelight, I can see each line on his face. Sometimes Harley seems like a big kid to me, but not tonight. Right now he's quiet and the creases around his eyes are dark and deep.

"Autumn . . ." He looks away. "I hope you're not angry with me."

I wait for him to go on, then realize it's a question.

"No. I'm sad, but I'm not angry. And I don't think you want to leave here any more than I do; I think you're just as sad as me."

"Autumn . . . I—"

"There are a lot of beautiful things about this island—like this house for one"—I straighten up and let the blankets fall around my lap—"and think about the herons and sunsets and big trees. You'd miss that, Harley."

"Autumn, it's not as if we're moving to Seattle. There are trees and herons and everything else on the big island, just like here."

He's right, of course.

"But it's not the same." I'm trying to think of a way to say this. "People over there live in big houses right next to one another and they have electric lights and televisions and garage door openers—"

"I don't think it's required that you have a garage door opener—"

"Uncle Bob does. And he smokes."

"Autumn, we won't live there long; I told you that. Just long enough to find our own place. Somewhere beautiful, just like this."

I know he's right; there are beautiful places on the big island. And he's trying so hard to make me happy. I wish I could tell him I'd be fine there, that I'm willing to make the best of it. That's what he came up here for, I imagine, to hear me say those words.

But I can't.

"Autumn, sometimes you have to grit your teeth and move on."

"Why?"

Harley rests his chin on his hands on the back of the chair and looks straight at me. "I don't have any retirement or anything. If I stop working, if I'm sick, the money stops. And we barely have enough to get by on as it is."

I heard all this yesterday morning at breakfast. And

how will he pay for college? And we're just wasting our money paying rent and people don't seem to be buying his stuff like they used to and so on. I wonder why Harley is so concerned with money all of a sudden.

"And your mother and I are having some problems. We're drifting apart, Autumn. I'll do anything to keep the three of us together. Anything. Even leave this island."

I have no idea what to say. Harley's words kind of hang there in space, waiting for me to really hear them.

After a while Harley says, "Good night," blows out the candle, and walks away. I listen to his moccasined feet pad down the dark stairway and then to the wind for a long time, trying not to think. A nearly full moon in the south sky shines between clouds, casting dark shadows across the floor and onto my bed.

When I finally sleep, I dream that the floor crumbles into nothingness beneath me and that I fall away.

I dream this over and over.

Tuesday

tuesday morning

low tide: 9:28 a.m.
barometer: 28.76; steady

I awaken and dress quickly. It's still dark. I pour a little water from the pitcher into the bowl and then splash some on my face. I check my backpack for the tenth time. Yes, everything is in there. I go downstairs. The kitchen stove is warm and the kettle sings quietly. Thanks, Harley, I think. I'm glad I don't have to wait for a fire to get roaring and settle down to coals before I can cook my breakfast. Harley's very good about this; he calls it "keeping the home fires burning." Mother sometimes forgets, but not Harley.

I make a cup of tea and slice some bread for toast. I decide to have French toast, so I get an egg from the pantry. As I stir the egg I wonder what Harley is doing out in his shop this morning and then I remember last night.

"I'll do anything to keep us together."

I cook the French toast on the griddle and eat it with butter and powdered sugar, the way Mother likes it, then quickly put the breakfast things away. I get water to do the dishes from the kettle and then refill it and put it on the back of the stove. I find a thick piece of madrone in the wood box and lay it on the coals. It will burn for hours. Harley will be in later for tea and he'll appreciate some hot water on a morning like this.

I put on my down jacket and wool hat, swing on the pack, grab my stick, and leave. The sky is overcast and the air smells like rain. The chimney smoke drifts lazily to the east in a long low line.

I set out.

The trail south follows the bay for fifty feet or so, then heads west into the trees. I catch glimpses of the water as I walk; it's dark and still. Soon I come to the fork and bear left and in no time I'm at the south dock. Then there's the zigzag path through the rocks to Jane's house. I'm surprised to find smoke coming from the chimney and Isis, her big white cat, on the porch.

Jane is home.

"Hi, Autumn," she yells as she opens the front door. Jane's wearing running shorts and a sweatshirt. "Come on in." I run up the steps and drop my pack and stick on the porch. Her arms are open and she hugs me tight.

"I just came to feed Isis," I tell her. "I didn't think you'd be home." The fireplace crackles and pops; there's music on and the smell of coffee.

"This early!" She laughs from the kitchen and returns with two cups of coffee. Mine has sugar and cinnamon. Drinking coffee is a little secret Jane and I share; Mother would never approve of such a thing. Jane sits cross-legged in the chair; I curl up on the couch. "Well, you needn't worry about that today. Isis is well fed and ready for action. Look out, mice!" She laughs again. Then, as if reading my mind, she says, "I had to get a few things. I guess we're going out for a couple of days to look at some orcas. I got a ride last night and the same boat is going back"—she cranes her neck to see the clock—"in about forty-five minutes. Some guy who has a cabin over by the airstrip. Nice guy, no imagination. Talked about the stock market all the way over." She smiles and sips her coffee.

Jane does this, comes back to the island sometimes during the week when she can get a ride. Since she's an intern, she's not expected to be at the museum at all hours like Mother. Mother says she's impulsive. I've known her to come home three times in one week and then not come home at all for a month. Harley says she floats through her life like a breeze. I've always wondered if that's a compliment or an insult.

Jane asks me how everything is going and gives no indication she knows Harley is planning to move us to the big island, so I tell her everything is fine and we talk about the season and the flowers and I show her my journal.

I want to tell her that it's more than a journal to me. I want to explain to her that Harley is in this book. And Forrest. And Mother. And her, and that everything I've drawn or will draw is something we've shared.

But I don't say that. I say something dumb like, Here's my journal. Jane seems impressed and says my drawings are beautiful.

I'll have to talk to her about leaving the island and about the reason I'm making this journal, but not now. I know I'll cry and she will, too, even though of course we'll still see each other. There is too much to say; it'll have to wait.

I sketch Jane while she gets herself ready and then we walk together down to the dock. The boat is waiting. A stern-looking man takes her bag. I steady the boat as she settles into the passenger seat, and before I can even say good-bye the nose of the boat lifts and they're off. I wait until she turns and waves and then I put on my backpack and walk away.

tuesday afternoon

high tide: 3:31 p.m.
barometer: 28.62; falling

Rain falls steadily out of the west. I tuck my braid and wisps of hair into the hood of my jacket and tighten it around my face. I pull on gloves. I should've worn jeans, or tights at least. Jane would've let me borrow some clothes.

I've been scrambling around up on the mountain all morning, looking at things, and I'm very wet. But Forrest will have a warm fire.

Once I get out on the headland, though, the rain comes in sheets. I bend into it. I can barely see and the wind is so strong I'm afraid it may blow me off the bluff. When I reach the little bench, I sit down to think. I'm closer to Forrest's house than anywhere else; it makes no sense to go back. But the rain and wind will be worse when I round the point.

Then I remember a path that follows the ravine from this bench up into the forest and crosses the island to the north. Harley and I have walked it several times in the past. It comes out somewhere near the lighthouse. And it goes through thick forest, which means less wind and rain.

Anything is better than this. I begin climbing. The trail follows a rivulet, which is dry during the summer but is now swirling and churning down the mountain. I can see shiny black bedrock through the water.

Soon I am up and out of the ravine and into the trees. At the edge of the forest I turn and look back upon the steel gray sea and sky. The tide's in. Three gulls soar above me, holding to the wind like kites tethered to the earth with invisible lines. Far to the south, two tankers leave V-shaped wakes, moving east. Harley hates the tankers; I'll never forget how he cried when he told me the story of the *Exxon Valdez*: a whole coastline buried in oil. It could happen here, he said.

I move on, into the forest. Under the thick canopy of fir trees the rain is more like mist and the air is suddenly silent. The movement of the treetops above is the only sign of the storm.

Soon the path forks and I choose to go uphill. I want to remain in the forest, not return to the sea and wind. But the path becomes difficult to follow, and now it's not really much of a path at all. Finally the land flattens out and the trail disappears altogether. I begin to feel like

I'm walking in circles. I backtrack and find there's no path there either, so I stop.

I have no idea where I am.

But I'm not lost. People get lost in vast wilderness, like Canada or Montana. You can't get lost on an island too small to have electricity or ferry service. People laugh about how small this place is: one of the green specks on the map near Seattle. How could I be lost?

Still . . . I don't know where the sea is from here. I can't remember a time on the island when I couldn't point instantly in the direction of the sea.

I listen. Nothing.

My heart pounds. I force myself to gaze around slowly in a complete circle, looking for anything that might help me know which way to go. In every direction is forest and undergrowth, red-barked madrones, dark maples, and big firs. Nothing looks familiar.

I sit down. I can't remember which way I came and I don't know what to do.

I fight the urge to set off in a blind rush into the undergrowth. Without a trail it would be slow going and who knows where I might end up.

I wonder what time it is. I try to add the time since I had lunch up on the mountain. I can hardly force myself to think. Come on, Autumn! How much time on the south trail? How much time sitting on the bench? I don't even know how long I've been sitting right here, let alone anything else.

It's after three, I'm sure. About four hours until dark. Maybe less. I try hard not to think about being stuck out here at night.

I remember I have waterproof matches and paper in

my backpack. I could probably start a fire, but who would see it? If Harley was looking for me, which he won't do until late tonight anyway, he'll look at Jane's house and he'll probably go to Forrest's after that and he might call for me along the trail, thinking I slipped off during the storm. But he'll never come up here. No one comes up here.

Harley has a whole bunch of funny little sayings. One of them is, "Hopelessly lost but making good time." I think it's a way for him to say he isn't sure if he's doing the right things with his life, but he's doing the best he can. At least that's how I always interpret it.

I am hopelessly lost but making *no* time and I simply cannot sit here any longer.

I can't be too far from the western side of the island, as the crow flies. If I walk south or west, I'm sure to be out of the woods before dark. But how to tell. There are no shadows, you can't figure out direction by where moss grows on trees, and of course I don't have a compass. The wind is steady out of the west in a storm like this, but I can't tell which way it's blowing.

Then I have an idea.

I put on my pack and begin to walk, trying to face into the wind. Before long I find what I'm looking for: an old blowdown—a big fir knocked down by some long-ago storm. Soon there's another. Both of them are lying in the same direction. That's good enough for me. Storms always come in from the ocean side; west must be where the roots are.

In a short time I'm on a deer trail moving west and downhill and then just before dark I'm descending a steep slope getting soaked by brush and grass and steady rain and caring not one bit. And just down the trail is a white cottage and the smell of alder smoke and the green-and-white beacon of the lighthouse circling silently overhead.

Wednesday

wednesday morning

low tide: 10:13 a.m.
barometer: 28.68; steady

I lie in bed with my grandmother's quilt pulled way up around me and I think about Equinox. Rain pounds against the western and southern windows, making the violet-blue morning a blur. On the east side, the trees dance in the wind and from time to time a branch sails by.

The storm is upon us.

In the house below I hear voices, Harley and Forrest, and the occasional careful clink of china. They're drinking tea, I suppose, trying to let me sleep. I think of them down there. Forrest talks about me surprising him last night, coming in out of the storm. How he let me wear his sou'wester on our walk home, how strong the wind was. Harley talks about moving to the big island. I imagine all this, of course; I can't really hear what they're saying.

It's comforting to hear voices, to have someone in the house on a day like this. Forrest is always good to have around; I'm glad we talked him into staying the night.

But today I wish it was Mother down there. Mother would have rescued the fragile things from the garden before the storm; she would have soup cooking; she would be planning some project for the afternoon.

Or Jane. How great it would be to wake up on a morning like this in Jane's loft. We'd light a big blaze in the fireplace, make a pot of coffee, and lie around in our nightshirts on the carpet, listening to reggae or Brazilian jazz or Lyle Lovett or something. I savor this thought for a moment, and then I think about Equinox again.

Equinox is a restaurant. A café is what Mother calls it. She goes there nearly every day, at least for tea, so everyone knows her. Whenever Mother and I are on the big island together, that's where we go for lunch. I have to dress up and they make a big fuss over me, which of course I hate. I like it best when Jane comes along; the waiters flirt with her and I get to be a pretty-much-ignored fourteen-year-old.

Equinox is a long, dark, narrow room with old brick walls. It's filled with little tables covered with white tablecloths. On every table is a candle and a small vase of fresh flowers. It's always full of customers, always noisy. Mother calls it "seriously European." Harley says it's a great place to spend twice as much money for half as much food. Not exactly his kind of place.

Last night, while I was drying off next to Forrest's stove, he sang a song about the equinox. Not the café but the position of the earth and sun.

I told him my story about nearly getting lost and said something like, "There certainly is a storm coming in." He smiled and took down his banjo and said yes, there certainly was. He said that the equinox was this Friday, and it was going to be a full moon, too. The rain didn't surprise him.

The storm blows outside my windows. I see Forrest settled into his big chair, the banjo in his lap, and hear him singing:

The equinox is a special thing,
First day of autumn, first day of spring,
Comes in March, September, too,
The earth is warm, the sky is blue.

Long ago, we used the sun for planting,
We watched it as it moved across the sky,
And when its rays were just exactly slanting
We sowed our seeds, we never questioned why.

Halfway between summer and December
In early fall there comes a time for rest,
Just before the harvest, we remember,
I have always loved this day the best.

There are fierce days of beginning and of ending,
There are times of birth and death and first and last,
But now is when the season's gently mending,
Let's live today, tomorrow comes too fast.

Forrest was silent after his song. He seemed to have forgotten I was there. After a while I said, for no reason, "Equinox is the name of a restaurant in Friday Harbor."

And Forrest said a peculiar thing. He said: "Equinox, yes. Linda's place, Linda and her . . . friends."

He said it in a funny way. Kind of a shaking-his-head, sad sort of way.

Linda's place, Linda and her . . . friends.

Why would he say that? I mean, why would he say it *that* way? In about three seconds he looked up and smiled and launched into another banjo tune and it was as though nothing had ever been said. But it was so strange.

And it made me remember something that happened in the restaurant not long ago.

Linda, of course, is my mother. It's always a little strange to hear her name; I call her Mother, Harley calls her honey, Jane calls her "your mom." Only Forrest calls her Linda.

About a month ago, after Harley and I got back from our last trip of the summer, Mother and I went shopping for school clothes and we ended up at Equinox for lunch. There was a cat hanging around outside the restaurant door, and I stopped to pet it before going in. So I was a few steps behind Mother as we entered the restaurant.

The chef, who is also the owner, was out of the kitchen, visiting people at tables, and when he saw Mother he decided to seat her himself. He gave her a little hug and said, "Where's your . . . friend?" He said "friend" exactly the same way Forrest did, with a pause, sort of making a big deal about it.

I walked up just in time to hear this and see Mother blush. There was just the slightest moment of awkward silence, both of them looking at me, and then Mother introduced me and we sat down to lunch as if nothing had happened.

I'd forgotten all about it. But this morning those words—and the way the chef said them—are seared into my brain and there's nothing I can do to get them out. They go together, somehow, those two phrases.

Linda and her . . . friends.

Where's your . . . friend?

Simple phrases that mean nothing and everything. And there's a third one I thought about on the way here last night, walking in the rain with Forrest. It goes with the other two:

Your mother and I are having some problems. We're drifting apart, Autumn.

I've heard these over and over in my head, all night, and I hear them now. Try as I might, I can't convince myself I'm making this up.

It makes too much sense.

So, I think about Equinox, about the dark café, and the candles, and the bookstore owners and writers and artists that eat there. About Mother all alone on the big island day after day, about late nights and the growing storm, and the sadness in Harley's eyes.

I think I finally get it.

I wish I didn't understand; I wish there was someone here I could talk to.

And most of all I wish I didn't see the image of a woman in the shape of my mother, far away across the water in a noisy café—right now, as I lie here alone in the storm, huddled under a green-and-blue quilt, my eyes filled with tears—a woman I hardly know, in a café called Equinox, sitting with a . . . friend.

❧

Harley is curled up on the futon with a cup of tea, pretty much exactly as I imagined he would be. He's drawing. He has a legal pad and a little plastic T square he uses to make straight lines. Forrest is sitting in the rocking chair, smoking his pipe and reading the nickel-ad paper we get every week. They both look up when they hear me on the stairs.

"Morning, Autumn," Harley says. I sure hope he can't tell what I'm thinking by looking at my face.

"Morning, Harley. Morning, Forrest." I hug them both quickly and go into the kitchen to get some breakfast. Oatmeal. Brown sugar, raisins. I cut a slice of bread and put it on the stove to toast. I'm afraid to go back out there. I can't imagine what I'll say. They're acting like it's just another day. They must know all about it. Probably everyone on the island knows all about it.

I feel like I'm going to explode and I'm sure they'll be able to see right through me, but I head to the living room with my breakfast and sit down. I resist the urge to just blurt out the whole thing and get it over with.

"What are you drawing, Harley?" I ask. Forrest folds the paper and looks up when I speak.

"Cabinets. I figure maybe once we get over to the big island I can design and build custom cabinets. There's lots more money in that kind of thing than in peddling crafts town to town." Harley keeps his eyes on his drawing.

We're about to move away from the most beautiful place in the world. And what is Harley thinking about?

Cabinets.

He's so serious, I don't know whether to laugh or cry. I almost choke on my toast. Suddenly I'm angry. Not at anyone, not even Mother. Just angry.

"Cabinets," I say.

"Lots of new construction over there," Forrest says. "Nice homes. People want fancy cabinets. Harley could make a lot of money, I bet."

"Making cabinets is pretty easy, compared to dulcimers," Harley mumbles.

Easy?

I look around at the dulcimers on the wall, at the rocking chair Harley made. A watery light comes in through the big windows. Harley's never talked about money like this before. He's never wanted things to be easy.

I look down at the floor, because I can't think of anything to say about cabinets. Harley goes back to drawing and Forrest picks up his paper and there's only the low whistle of the kettle and the gentle thunking of Sidecar's tail as he wags it in his sleep. There are two holes in the floor where Harley once tried to install a large antique gas pump. He rented a dinghy and towed the pump all the way from Orcas Island. He and two other men took an entire day to roll it on a cart up the hill from the dock and bolt it to the floor here in the living room. Harley was so excited to get the pump, he ignored the gas fumes until Mother came home from work two days later. By that time, the cabin smelled like a truck stop and Mother was, as Harley puts it, "less than pleased," and he had to take the pump out, roll it down the hill, and tow it back to Orcas.

Remembering this reminds me of how much I love Harley's stories. Like the time he got stuck all night in a tree when he sawed off the wrong branch, or when he was chased twice in one day by the same bees, or the time he rolled my uncle's truck into the bay. I imagine he could tell stories all night and never share the same one twice.

I want to tell him how much I love his stories, but I say, "Why can't you make cabinets right here?"

Harley stops working and looks over his yellow pad at me. Forrest looks over at Harley and then at the floor. There's a long silence. "Autumn—"

I don't even let him get started. "This island is as important to you as it is to me! I don't think you can be happy anywhere else!"

"It's not—"

I don't want to hear it all over again. "I know," I snap, "it's not like we're moving to Seattle! But it's not like living here either."

Harley watches me. His T square is poised in midair. Forrest waits. I wait for Harley's next line. I wait for him to say we'll find some land away from the crowds, a place much like this one.

But he doesn't say that. He says, very softly, "You're right, Autumn. I've thought long and hard about it, believe me." Forrest clears his throat as if to speak and Harley shoots him a glance. "I still think it's the best thing for us, all of us, to move to the big island.

Autumn, there are some things you just can't understand."

That does it! I look down at my empty plate and let it clatter carelessly onto the coffee table. Harley, I think, there are things *you* just don't understand! After everything I have been through in my mind this morning, that's about the last thing I want to hear. I need to lash out; to say something awful. What I really want to say is: Mother's got some boyfriend in Friday Harbor and everyone seems to know about it but me!

But I don't. Instead I say, "You can make me go if that's what you want, Harley! I just hope you've thought about how this will ruin my life."

And before either of them can move or speak I grab my coat and backpack and run out into the storm.

wednesday afternoon

high tide: 4:13 p.m.
barometer: 28.56; falling

I'm using a field guide to make a sketch of a raven. Rain sweeps in waves across the windshield of the old abandoned pickup truck where I've come to work and think. Inside the cab it's dry and comfortable.

No one knows how this old pickup truck with its flat tires and missing engine ended up on this grassy hillside. There's no road to this spot; it's the only automobile on the island.

The truck is a landmark—everyone knows about it. People use it to give directions. Over near the old truck, they say. You can see it from out in the strait as you come across from Friday Harbor if you know where to look.

People eat lunch in the cab. I mean, they come here on purpose to have a picnic. Jane comes to write in her journal. I suppose people must come here, like I do, just to look out over the forest and the sea. It's a beautiful view.

Inside, it's neat and clean except for the dashboard. Each time people visit the truck they leave something as a reminder that they were there. So the metal dashboard is covered with coins, shells, rocks, and many other treasures.

I think my favorite thing about the truck is a little white statue of the Virgin Mary, which stands in the exact center of the dashboard. She seems to rise directly out of the clutter. Harley told me this statue was probably attached to the truck when it came here.

I look at the figurine and wonder, as I always do, what she's doing in the truck, way up on this mountain. I think of the time passing (Harley says that the truck is a 1947 Dodge), the little white statue silent and alone year after year. *Solstice-equinox-solstice-equinox-solstice . . .*

I think of Jane. She's alone, too. I mean, she has me, of course, and she has friends at work. Her parents live

in Los Angeles. But when she's here on weekends she's always alone, just her and Isis. I asked her once if she wanted to get married and she laughed and looked away.

I'm like that, too, I suppose. Alone, I mean. The only kids my age on the island are Mark and Henry, dull farm boys who live on the other side, by the airport. They don't even go to school. There's a seventeen-year-old girl named Alicia over on the north side. We speak when we run into each other, but she seems more interested in her fingernails and makeup than anything else. She's waiting until she's eighteen so she can move away to a city somewhere. She doesn't go to school either.

The kids who do go to school are all younger than me; the oldest is ten. I often feel more like Ms. Crosby's helper than a student. I like school even though I don't always go.

Jane is the only person I can really call a friend. We couldn't have gotten to know each other like we have if she had a boyfriend hanging around, or other women her age.

I look at the statue and wonder if I could talk to Jane about Mother's lover on the big island. Maybe she could help me understand it. She works with Mother every day, after all.

Here and there in some of Mother's books I have seen little notes in the margin or in the white space above a poem. *Linda, this is you! . . . Line 12 . . . Remember last month . . .* Things like that, written in black ink, in handwriting I don't recognize, always the same. I never thought about them until now.

I wonder if Jane *would* tell me the truth, if she knew, or if she would lie to make me feel better.

Once, a few years ago, I decided to take the statue home with me. I thought that surely she would be happier in my warm room than here. I reached out and wrapped my hand around her. Just then, a raven flew over, making his loud throaty cry. I pulled my hand back as quickly as if I'd been bitten by a snake. When I slid over to the window to look, the raven was gone. I've never forgotten that moment. I left the statue where it was.

I find a scrap of paper in my backpack and make a quick drawing of a raven, like the one I've just completed in my journal, fold it, and place it on the dashboard with everything else. I put away my stuff and open the door to find the rain has stopped and there are silver glints in a metal gray sky.

"Let's make a cover for your journal," Forrest says, almost before I get in the door. "Then I want to see what you've been working on."

He takes my coat and points me toward the counter, where he has all the materials for making paper. He's succeeded in surprising me and I can tell this pleases him. "I've been waiting all afternoon for you to show up," he says.

A cover. This idea has never occurred to me. True, my journal is very plain on the outside, just black, but it's the inside I've been thinking about, filling up with images and words, just the way I had hoped. I'm very pleased with it and had never given a thought to the outside.

"Here's some tea," Forrest says, "and here are some maple leaves and grasses, some lichen and other things. And of course flowers." He moves these into my reach as he talks. "Wonderful," he says, "let's get started."

A warm rectangle of sunlight, very welcome after all the rain, stretches across the counter as Forrest and I tear up old practice drawings, first drafts of journal entries, and other scraps of paper into narrow strips. We drop them into the kettle.

"What's in there?" I ask.

"Water mostly. Cornstarch, a few other things."

I'm taken by the idea of making a paper cover now and want to think of nothing else. I push all the dark thoughts into the back of my head. They'll wait.

Forrest keeps fussing with everything and arranging neat little piles of leaves and things and this makes me laugh. "You don't suppose any of this"—I wave a stack of drawings I don't like—"will show up in the paper, do you?"

"You mean one of your disasters right there on the cover of your journal for the rest of your life?" We laugh. "No chance of that," he says. "You'll see."

Forrest shows me how to tear up the plants and leaves—not too small, he says. All this goes into the kettle.

"We need some color in there," Forrest blurts out suddenly, looking around in his kitchen. "I wonder what I have."

"Color?" I imagine a bright pastel book jacket. "You mean, like food coloring?"

"No, like flecks. Like colored paper. We need some accents to make it more interesting." Forrest is searching through stacks of books now.

Colored paper. I remember something. I pull the field guide out of my backpack. Inside the front cover are several pages advertising other field guides: insects, flowers, and so on. One is sort of a magenta, another is green and blue. "Like this?" I ask, holding open the book.

Forrest is down on his knees looking through the bottom shelf of his bookcase. He turns and smiles. "Perfect!"

I rip the pages out and tear them into strips. "Pick one and put it all in," he says. "That will give us a background color. Drop in a few pieces of the others. They'll be flecks here and there." I choose magenta for color and blue and green for the flecks. The paper is turning into a thick soup; it looks terrible. Forrest tosses in a piece of blue yarn he's found. "Why not?" he says with a shrug.

It smells worse than it looks. Yuck.

Before long, Forrest is pouring the contents of the kettle into a strainer and then the pinkish goop from the strainer into a frame with a piece of mesh attached to it. We form the goop into a large flat square and push with our hands until water stops dripping into the pan below. With most of the water squeezed out, I can begin to see what the paper will look like.

Flecked with color, filled with bits of leaves and flowers, it's lovely. Grasses and individual strands of yarn swirl throughout, forming dark accents. I want to wrap it around my book immediately, I like it so much. But there's more to do.

"Let's tip it—gently!—out of there, onto this flower press," Forrest says. Then we attach the top of the press. Now the paper is between two boards. At each corner is a wing nut. We take turns twisting these, keeping the pressure even, and colored water oozes out of the press and pools on the counter. I can sense the paper getting drier and flatter and more beautiful with every turn.

"This will be fine," Forrest says. "After a while, I'll take it out and hang it above the stove to dry completely. And it'll be a lot flatter and sleeker looking than if we hadn't used the press. Most people would just squeeze out the water with their hands or a board or something, and let it go at that. I've always liked using the press. Kind of my little secret."

The sun slants in. I think of the paper, dry and flat in the flower press.

"It'll still be rough—that's what we want—but it will be earthy and real and all that, of course, but, I don't know, what would you call it?" Forrest asks, searching for the right word.

"Sleek," I say, shouldering my backpack, "sounds like a seal." I have to laugh. "I would call it wonderful."

"Yes," he says, laughing out loud, "that's it. That's the exact word I was looking for. Wonderful."

wednesday night

low tide: 11:07 p.m.
barometer: 28.51; falling

The house is empty when I return before dark. There's potato soup on the stove. This and some tea make my supper. When I'm finished I decide I'll curl up in my bed and read before I sleep. As I browse through the lower shelves of the bookcase, I remember the photo albums.

There are three on the top shelf, filled with pictures of my parents when they were young. I haven't seen those pictures in a long time. I stand on a stool to reach the albums, then squeeze them under my arm as I head upstairs so I can carry a cup of tea in the other hand. Harley comes into the house just as I get settled. I hear him moving around downstairs and remember I was angry with him this morning. He'll come up soon, I tell myself. I'll apologize then.

The photos of Mother are what catch my eye. I look at each picture, page after page. Harley looked about the same then as he does now. Mother, though, is like a completely different person. She is young and thin, with dark curly hair nearly to her waist. She is tanned and pretty and smiling in every picture. The photos were taken before I was born.

Mother came west from Pennsylvania. Her aunt and uncle had taken care of her after her parents died and she left "the day they turned their backs on her," according to Harley. I guess her aunt and uncle were pretty strict.

Looking at these old pictures, I get the impression that Mother was a little wild after she left Pennsylvania. There's even one photo where her bare bottom is turned to the camera, with Harley and some other guys standing around smiling. Mother is looking over her shoulder, laughing. Someone, maybe Harley, has written *crazy Linda* across the lower corner of the photo.

"Beautiful girl." My heart skips a beat; I wonder how long Harley's been standing in the doorway. "May I come in?"

"Sure," I say. I start to close the album, but he's there, pulling up the old chair, swinging it around backward, and reaching down to touch a picture, all in one motion. The photo is of Mother sitting cross-legged on the deck of a boat, her hair flowing down around her.

"That was our little sailboat. We went everywhere in that."

"Is that here?" I ask.

"No," he says absently. "In Port Townsend." Of course. They didn't move here until I was about two.

He positions the album so it's between us and names the people in the pictures: Phil, Donna, Jean. A dog, Blitz. And then, suddenly, there's a photo of Mother holding a baby. I had no idea there were any pictures of me in here.

"How old am I there?"

Harley laughs. "You hadn't come along yet. That's the neighbor's kid. I can't remember his name."

On the next page is a series of photos of Mother posing in a yellow one-piece swimsuit. She looks like a model in a magazine.

"She's pregnant there," Harley says. "You're in there, but she doesn't know it yet." So I *am* in these albums, in a way. It seems odd that Harley would remember something like that. There are almost no photographs of me, not as a little kid and not now. Mother and Harley don't own a camera anymore. Jane has taken some pictures of me, but that's only been in the last two years.

"She doesn't look pregnant."

"Well, it was early. Nothing to see yet."

And then for some reason I try to be funny, so I say, "Well, I sure was a beautiful baby. Any more pictures of me like this?" It's supposed to be a joke. But it comes out all wrong, so it isn't funny and neither of us laugh.

Harley is silent, staring into space.

Without looking he says, "I think I made you mad this morning, Autumn, telling you there were some things you can't understand. I'm sorry. You're older now. I forget sometimes. I didn't mean to hurt your feelings." I start to apologize, but he keeps going. "So, I'm not going to say that again. I'll just answer your question.

"It's kind of a long story, but it goes like this: When your mother found out she was pregnant with you, right after these pictures were taken, she ran away. Just disappeared one night. I didn't know what to do. I drove all over town, looking for her. I went to the police."

Harley stands up and walks over to the window. I pull the quilt around me.

"You have no idea how awful it is when someone you love just disappears. No one does. I mean, most people at least get some warning, or someone leaves a note, or there's a phone call, or something. She just disappeared, Autumn; I woke up and she was gone.

"I waited for her; I put candles in the window; I stayed home almost every night in case she came back. I left a note on the door when I was gone so she would know I was still around. Winter came, and then spring. I became numb, finally. The weeks and months went by and in the middle of summer, when I had finally given up hope, she came back. One night there was a knock on the door and she was there. Holding you."

I wait to hear the rest of the story; Harley looks out into the night. I can think of nothing to say, so I ask, "Why?"

"Why'd she run away? I'm still not sure, Autumn. Maybe she just wasn't ready to be a mother; she was awful young. Barely eighteen. Maybe she was looking for someone better than me. We were just friends, really, before . . . before you came along. We'd only known each other a few months. I don't know."

Friends. A few months.

"Sometimes I think your mother thought she'd come out west and it would be one continuous party. She had a picture of this in her mind. She graduated from high school, hitchhiked out here, and before the summer was over she was pregnant. Maybe when she found out, she panicked. She just ran without thinking, I guess."

"Where'd she go?"

"I don't know."

In my belly I feel something like cold metal. I hear the quiet pain in Harley's voice. I feel myself unraveling, knowing more than I want to know.

I think about my father, crazy with fear and worry,

never knowing where his beautiful girl and their baby had gone.

"You never asked her?"

He leans against the windowsill and folds his arms across his chest. I know what he's going to say. We wait in silence for a moment.

"No. She was a lot different when she came back, nothing like those pictures. I never asked her. She wasn't the same Linda I had known. I was never sure she really wanted to be with me."

He says this last thing as if it has become an ordinary part of his life. *I was never sure she really wanted to be with me.*

"But she came back and had you with her and that was enough."

I wait a long time until the lump in my throat gets a little smaller and I manage to ask, "Then what, after she came back?"

"We didn't get married or anything, but I made a promise I would keep our family together. We needed each other." Harley turns to look at me. "I made that promise to myself, Autumn, and I was thinking about you. She disappeared with you once; I don't think I could stand it happening again. Everything I've done since that time I've done to keep us together, you and me. That's the most important thing of all; it is now and it was then. I worked in a sawmill for a while and saved some money and then we came here, to the island. It seemed like a good place for a family."

Seemed.

"We've kind of led our separate lives here, your mother and I. It hasn't been easy, but it's worked pretty well up to now."

Harley pulls his hair back into a ponytail and tries to smile. I let him tuck the covers around me and kiss me on the forehead and then take the photo albums downstairs. A big moon moves slowly out of the fir trees and into the south sky. I blow out the lamp and lie in the darkness for a long time.

Sobbing.

Thursday

thursday morning

low tide: 10:59 a.m.
barometer: 28.65; *steady*

The morning, when it comes, is bright and clear, with a strong, steady wind out of the southwest. Harley is once again clearing out his shop, stacking boxes and wood and tools on the porch. I watch through the kitchen window and drink my tea. When he brings out an old bucket filled with smooth dark logs I'm reminded of a winter day a few years ago.

Harley and I worked in an abandoned pear orchard, cutting off the dead wood and pruning back the trees. It was sunny, like now, and our breath came out in clouds. We hauled all the usable wood down to his shop in a wheelbarrow. It was fun, just the two of us, laughing and playing word games. I remember Harley talking with an Irish accent: "Aye, lass," he would say, "and would ye be a-wantin' a wee bit o' lunch, now?" Harley's very good with accents. He'd twist up his face to go with the accent and I laughed until my belly hurt.

And now there's a bucket of pear wood on the porch of his shop.

I'm determined to look at things today, to walk around with my journal, to find some high place where I can look down on my island and the sea.

I wash my teacup and put it in the drainer, gather my things, and go out. Sidecar is there, wiggling all over, wanting me to pet him. I stroke his neck and in a moment Harley appears at the shop door with a saw in each hand. We just kind of stand there looking at each other, planning what we're going to say and not say, I suppose.

"Radio says the storm's gonna hit hard this afternoon. You be careful coming home."

"I thought it was over," I say. The sky is blue.

"No. This is sort of like the eye of a hurricane. Big winds and rain still to come. Tonight. Barometer's been falling just about all week."

And it's the equinox and a full moon tomorrow, I remember.

"Bye, Harley." Halfway down the trail I stop and turn around. He's watching me, his ragged red-and-black work coat flapping in the wind.

"I'll be careful!" I yell, finally, then turn and walk away.

And before I've gone another hundred yards I nearly

run into Forrest, who is ambling along, hands in pockets, puffing on his pipe, my paper under his arm.

⚘

I'm going to feed Jane's cat, but first I want to sit on a rock at the very edge of the island, hear the water moving all around me, and feel the yellow sun on my face.

I fold the handmade paper around my journal. It seems nearly alive, so rich with grasses and flowers, and more beautiful than I imagined.

I look across the water to San Juan Island and think about Mother. I remember her smell, and if I close my eyes I can see her moving in the garden. I think about her dark eyes and the shape of her face.

I sketch the green island shimmering across the channel, and the sailboats, and wonder what she's doing right now. I want to talk to her, to have her tell me everything I need to hear. I want to be a part of her life like I am a part of Harley's life.

But Mother's over there until tomorrow and the tide's coming back in, so I get up, put my journal carefully into my backpack, pick up my stick, and walk up the beach.

⚘

Isis is waiting just inside the door; she arches her back and rubs against my leg. Lunchtime. I pour food into the bowl and give her fresh water.

I get a fire going and Jane's cabin warms up right away. I like being here. Thin dappled sunlight moves on the wall and the house smells like wood smoke. There's a George Winston tape in the cassette player, so I turn it on. I make lunch with some French bread, sharp cheese, and an apple, and I sit in the big chair with a blanket over my legs, listening to piano music, eating, and looking out at the bay.

Jane went to college in Vermont, and she travels to Europe when she can. We often talk about her work—the whales—and the island. We laugh a lot. But I don't really know much about her past, or her life when she's not here with me.

I decide to finish eating my apple in the loft. There's a ladder made of pale wood and in a moment I'm at the top. I've always loved Jane's bedroom. Tucked in a corner of the house, hidden from below by a low wall, it's like a little nest, filled mostly with a big futon mattress and shelves all around. Jane's things from Italy, her magazines, and her clothes are everywhere.

Through the skylight I'm surprised to see dark clouds and a few drops of rain; the storm has returned.

I sit on her bed and notice a black box I've never seen before. It isn't exactly hidden, just kind of pushed back behind the books.

I move the paperbacks aside and carefully pick up the box. There's a little silver heart holding the box shut, with a keyhole in its center.

I touch the heart and the lid clicks open. Immediately the box begins to play music and I see that the silver heart is not a lock but the place where the music box is wound.

Inside the box are photographs.

A hard rain falls on the skylight as I look at the pictures. Photographs of two lovers; one of them is my mother.

The other is Jane.

For a moment I'm frozen. Then I drop the box and stumble down the ladder and out the front door.

I follow the old homestead fence until I get to the path and when I'm out of the forest and high on the bluff I run. Headlong into the storm.

thursday afternoon

high tide: 4:56 p.m.
barometer: 28.42; falling

The tiny bay just north of the lighthouse is like a bowl carved into the rocky cliff. North and south of here, the sea moves against sheer black cliffs where seabirds make their nests in spring. But in here is a circle of cobble beach surrounding an immense flat black rock. The ocean flows in and out, moving in slow flat waves around the rock, rolling the round stones on the beach with a hollow, musical sound that echoes from the walls above.

From the rock I watch the white walls of surf pour into the bay, flatten out, then slide back into the sea, again and again.

Since not one thing in my life bears even the slightest resemblance to the way I imagined things were a week ago, about the only thing I can do is build a little hut where I can't be found and live alone until I'm old. Or maybe a hollow tree like the boy did in *My Side of the Mountain.*

Mother and Jane . . .

I need to imagine them together, with friends and

alone in the dark. I need to feel, somehow, their affection for each other and to know most of all that it does not include me. And I need to find them together in the shadow of my memory—taking moonlit walks, exchanging knowing smiles—and bring them into the light; I have to let them be real.

Someday.

But not now; I'm too scared even to begin.

I wrap my arms around myself to keep warm. I have nowhere to go. But I can't sit on this cold rock any longer, so I stand and begin to walk back and forth. My hair blows and the spray covers me like a mist. There's a sound I haven't noticed until now, a steady roar. It's the wind blasting over the cliffs above me.

I walk back and forth a few more times, trying unsuccessfully to think of nothing, and when the sound of the wind gets even louder and I can't tell anymore where the sea ends and the sky begins, I climb down the rock and find water.

Blue-black water that sways and dances, marked with crossing patterns of white foam. Water that circles lazily around the rock, gurgling, finding new places to splash up onto the black stone, rushing back, then returning to run into the low places, each time a little higher. Dark storm water, hissing and sucking.

The wind and moon have caused the water to come into the little bay and now the cobble beach and the tide pools are gone and there's nothing but steep stone walls and moving water and the rock itself, like a shrinking island. And me.

The tide has come in.

I could wade over if I go right now. Or I could swim. I'd have to leave my clothes and backpack here and it would be cold. But it's only fifty feet to solid ground and then I could run to Forrest's house and warm up.

But the water is so dark. And it moves strangely, as if there are currents below. And now the wind is even stronger, whistling overhead, and the bay is choppy.

I'm afraid to get in the sea. I'm afraid I'll be swept away. My mind tells me to go, but I can't. I can only sit with my knees tucked under my chin, and watch.

Soon the sea is at my feet. I pick up my stick and backpack and climb up to the highest part of the rock. The sky darkens until it's like night and the wind roars through the opening in the cliff.

Maybe the water will stop.

It's so dark now I can only sense the water rising and then suddenly it's around me, touching me like death itself, and I'm screaming, but the wind tears the sound out of my mouth. I feel my skirt billowing around me in the icy water and still I sit hugging my knees, the sea lapping at me.

I know I am clinging to the rock, and the sea is rising around me, but now everything is clear. I allow myself to be wrapped in a blue cocoon where I'll be safe and warm forever.

I feel myself drifting, sliding down into warm slumber, snuggling into the soft blue cocoon. When I wake, I'll be a butterfly.

And then I am floating off the rock, floating away, and there is something very near my face and I hear a voice. Autumn, Autumn, says the voice, and I hold on and wrap the rope all around me like the voice says, and I drift away from the rock, out into the sea, and I cry for the butterfly I will never become and for the simple island life I thought would be mine forever.

Equinox

Once, when I was about seven, Harley decided to take the three of us to Disneyland. We rode the ferry to Anacortes, borrowed an old van from someone, and made it clear into Oregon before he got disgusted with the whole idea and turned around.

Then the van broke down. While we were waiting for a mechanic to come to the rest area, Harley put on his court-jester outfit and juggled and did acrobatics for other travelers. Soon he had a crowd and they were all putting money in his jar.

The police came and made him stop. Harley called them names and argued with them, and he got the other people to do the same.

Before long, Harley was in jail and Mother and I were in a motel and the van was at a gas station. By the time we got back to the island all the Disneyland money was gone and Harley had to do odd jobs to pay for the repairs to the van.

Mother, who didn't want to go in the first place, didn't speak for weeks.

Harley used to tell the Disneyland story to anyone who'd listen; for him it was just another adventure. "We didn't need to go clear to California to find Mickey Mouse and Goofy," he would say. "They came to us in a big white car with lights on top!" Harley could sure make people laugh, telling that story.

Forrest is moving around in the kitchen, behind me, and I'm pretending to be asleep, wrapped in a sleeping bag on the floor. Sunlight pours into the house; it's late morning. My clothes are dry and folded by the stove, and there's my backpack, and the rope Forrest used to pull me out of the ocean, coiled and hung on its hook by the banjo.

"So, how about some breakfast?" he says.

I guess I'm not fooling him. I turn and snuggle into the sleeping bag. I'm embarrassed to have been caught by the tide and grateful he saved me, but there's nothing I can say right now that won't sound ridiculous.

So I answer, "Sure," and sit up.

"I'm going out for a few minutes," he says, and looks from me to my clothes and back. I take the hint and when he comes back in I'm dressed and sitting at the table with a cup of tea.

"Well," he says, "that was quite a blow. You picked a fine day to go swimming."

"Yeah, I really wanted to go sailing, but there wasn't enough wind."

We don't laugh.

"How'd you know where I was?" I ask finally. "I was supposed to be lost."

He puts scrambled eggs and biscuits on the table and we eat.

"Followed you," he says with a sheepish grin. I wonder how many times he's followed me around in the past, checking to make sure I was okay. "I was up on the trail there, coming back from your place, and saw you run out of Jane's house like you were going to a fire. I went down there and found the door open, so I . . . well, I snooped around a little. I was pretty curious to see what would make you run out like that." Forrest gives me a look. "I heard a little music playing up in the loft and when I climbed up there and found what you found, well, I thought I'd better keep an eye on you, staying pretty far behind, of course.

"I got clear around on the north side before I figured out I'd lost you somehow, so I worked my way back, looking. I thought the last place you'd be in such a storm was down in that hole, but I looked anyway, and there you were. I came back here, figuring you'd sit there and stew for a while and then come here and we'd have dinner together and all that, talk things over. It started getting dark, though, and that big tide was coming in and the wind was howling, and you still weren't here. I thought you must have gone home. But I headed up that way, just in case; at the last minute I grabbed the rope." He says, dead serious now, his eyes right on me, "That was pretty close, Autumn."

Yeah, I know.

It feels good to be on solid ground, maybe better than it's ever felt before.

I want to say something, but I don't know how. Finally he asks, "Are you all right?" and I understand he's asking not about the storm but about Mother.

And then I just blurt out, "I have no idea how I'm going to keep it from Harley. He'll take one look at me and—"

"Harley knows."

"You told him?" I ask, amazed. I imagine Forrest walking back to our house in the rain and saying, Oh, by the way, I found some interesting pictures of your wife and Jane.

"No, he told me."

"B-But, Forrest," I stutter, "I—"

"Autumn, I'm a real bad liar and you're a real smart girl and you might just as well know the truth. That relationship has been going on for quite a while. Harley always figured it wasn't his place to tell you about it, and I guess Jane and your mom thought you didn't need to know. Looks like you found out on your own."

"You mean, Jane—"

"Your mom got her a job at the museum so they could be together. And Jane had her house built close to yours. That wasn't a coincidence either, Autumn."

"And Harley knows all about this."

"Yeah, he does. I mean, he doesn't ask a lot of questions; I don't imagine it's something he and your mom talk about much. But he knows."

"You mean, not only is my mother having an affair with a girl who I thought was my friend, but my father just lets it happen? He waves good-bye every Monday as they sail away together? He listens to lots of old records while they work late in Jane's cabin? He doesn't even care?"

"Harley—"

"—is too laid-back for his own good!"

"—has thought for a long time, trust me. He's doing what he thinks is best for you; not for himself or Linda. You."

A little light goes on in my head. "And that's why we're moving to San Juan."

"You might say that. Harley's just trying to keep his family together."

"So it has nothing to do with making cabinets."

"No."

"Or retirement."

"No."

"But how's moving over there supposed to make anything better?" I ask.

Forrest looks down and pokes around on his plate. "Autumn, I've said too much already; I—" He takes a quick look at me and then sighs and looks out at the sea. "Linda has decided to move to the big island full-time. She wants to take you with her."

So that's it.

Forrest turns to look at me. "Autumn, your father loves this island as much as you do. You know that. After a while, people just become part of a place. It gets inside you in some powerful way. Harley doesn't want to move to San Juan, but he has to do something. He can't just let Linda take you away."

"What if I don't go?"

"What do you mean," he asks, "are you going to live here with me?"

"What if I decide to stay here with Harley?"

"Harley's moving to San Juan."

"He'll stay if I do. He told me he wanted to keep us together more than anything. The two of us, he said."

"Autumn, believe me, if your mother decides to take you with her, there's nothing you or Harley can do about it. So he's doing the only thing he can think of, following Linda over there, hoping it'll all work out somehow."

"What if it doesn't?" I'm thinking of Mother and Jane, late night cafés and art galleries and dinner parties, and I'm thinking Harley just doesn't get it.

"He hasn't let himself think that far yet."

Forrest gets up and begins to clear the dishes. I walk over and take the journal out of my backpack. I've been keeping it in a sealed plastic bag so it's dry, even after my swim. I turn the pages, one at a time, flattening them.

"What about Mother? What does she think?"

"She's already told you," he says over his shoulder, from the kitchen. "She's ambivalent. Harley says she's not real excited about him coming along, but she hasn't said no. You know how she is."

Which means it won't work.

"It doesn't matter, Autumn, what she thinks or what Harley thinks. There's nothing you can do about that.

You can't change the situation; about the only thing you can change is the way you deal with it."

Yeah, like finding a hollow tree.

"Forrest," I say after a minute, "help me. What can I do?"

"Autumn," he begins, "I can't—"

But I'm next to him now; my hand is on his arm. He stops drying a cup and looks at me.

"Forrest, I'm asking."

He sighs and carefully puts the cup away, then leans against the counter, folding and refolding the towel. We face each other across the little kitchen and for a time there's only the ticking of the clock and hissing of the kettle.

"You have a family," Forrest says quietly, "that loves you very much, each in their own way, and I'm counting Jane in there, too. You probably want to think about that. Good families are pretty hard to find; it doesn't really matter where they live or what they're shaped like." We look at each other, look away, then look at each other again. "Love is more rare than you might imagine, Autumn, and there's not enough of it to go around. If I were you, since you're asking, I'd start there and see where it goes."

I hoist the backpack onto my shoulder and move to

the open doorway. It's warm, almost like summer again; the sky is deep blue.

Forrest smiles kindly. We're thinking the same thing, of course, something I've been thinking pretty much all morning, something I believe I've known all along. I let him put my thoughts into words. "You probably ought to go save Harley from himself before it's too late," he says.

friday afternoon

high tide: 5:47 p.m.
barometer: 30.12; steady

The island waits; it's a clear, perfect day exactly halfway between summer and winter. Equinox. The last of the flying insects and the distant seaplanes hum, and tourist boats are everywhere.

When the *Wind Spirit* comes booming into the bay Jane is riding on the deck, her blond hair blowing around like a flag in the wind, and I'm standing at the edge of the south dock.

They wave and I see them laugh. Mother cuts back on the throttle and the Chris-Craft settles into the blue water, drifting slowly toward me in the golden sunlight.

When Mother steps onto the dock, I think she can see that I know. Her eyes are full. And the hurtful, silly words I might have said yesterday or a few hours ago do not come.

Instead, we face each other, and she puts her hands on my shoulders. After a moment she says, very quietly, "We'll be okay no matter what, Autumn, you and I. But you've been here all these years and now . . . it won't be long till you're grown," she whispers. "Please, Autumn."

The island waits in the autumn afternoon, and I am here now, and I will be here always.

"Yes," I say. "Yes. We'll be okay."

No matter what.

Epilogue

Nov. 15
Equinox
Friday Harbor

Dear Harley,

How are you? Your letter sounded pretty lonely. You know I'd run right over there if I could, but I'll be there Friday as usual. Only two more days.

I'm sitting in the café as I do now every morning, waiting for a couple of the other art students to arrive. Mother and Jane were here earlier, but they've gone off to work. When the other kids arrive we'll have a mocha or something and share our latest

projects, then walk together to the magnet school. I still can't get used to calling it that—I always get a picture in my mind of a big metal thing.

Yesterday a new girl joined our morning

coffee group, Adriana. Some artist wrote her
a letter to get her in, just like Forrest wrote
one for me. Everyone here thinks
Forrest is quite the big deal,
you know, illustrating those
chichi expensive books we laugh about, and
the children's books, and being a big-shot art
professor back in the sixties and all that. I
never stop hearing about it.

Anyway, Adriana will be a junior. She
works in watercolor. She showed me her
portfolio. It's pretty amazing. Lots of
flowers. No wonder she got in. Her parents
live in—guess where—Port Townsend! She lives
with her aunt during the week and goes home
on weekends and vacations like me.

Anyway, I had to tell her the whole story
of how my journal, with Forrest's help, got
me into the magnet school and how it's
going to be my freshman project and
everything.

I have a couple of new things in there

since last weekend. I can't wait
to show them to you. One is a
heron I saw in a marsh just
outside of town. It looks sort
of like this one.

   Mother and I went
for a walk
Monday night
and there it was.
My teacher says I
should put things from
both islands—both of my lives, he said—in
my journal. He thinks it will have more
texture, whatever that means.

   You asked if Mother is happy. I think so.
You know how sometimes she doesn't tell you
exactly; you kind of have to guess. But our
little yellow house is starting to feel more like
home finally, and Jane has most of her stuff
moved in upstairs and I think Mother is glad
everything is out in the open now. She seems
more relaxed. Last night we sat on the couch

together for the longest time and read sonnets
and just talked. I'm getting to know her in a
new way.

There's a lot to like here, but I miss you.
Sometimes I think about you and Sidecar all
by yourselves over there and the misty
mountain and the winter birds and Forrest
and it's all I can do to keep myself from
jumping in the first boat I can find and
heading home.

But we all promised, didn't we? A year,
we'd try this for a full year. I'm not sure how
I'll feel next autumn, next equinox, when it's
time to decide.
We'll see.

For now,
here's a
sketch. It's
me sitting
at this table,
reflected in
the front

window of the café. The sky is gray, the last of the leaves swirl about, and it is good to be in where it's warm.

I love you.

Autumn